It's not fair

For Clare Coggins with love – ED

Created exclusively for World International Limited by Bloomsbury Publishing Plc
First published in Great Britain in 1997 by World International Limited, Deanway
Technology Centre, Wilmslow Road, Handforth, Cheshire SK9 3FB

Copyright © Text Elizabeth Dale 1997
Copyright © Illustrations Lisa Smith 1997
Art Direction Lisa Coombes

The moral right of the author and illustrator has been asserted
A CIP catalogue record of this book is available from the
British Library

ISBN 0 7498 3092 1

Printed by Bath Press, Great Britain

10 9 8 7 6 5 4 3 2 1

Little Readers

It's not fair

Elizabeth Dale

Pictures by Lisa Smith

World International Limited

It just wasn't fair! Harry stared at the sock with the hole in it made by Marcus. And the jeans with the large paint stain left by Johnny.

And the jumper that had been **stretched** by George.

"Hand-me-down Harry,
that's me!" said Harry, miserably. "It's not fair!"

"Come on, Harry!" called Harry's mum.
"We've got to take your brothers to school!"

And she
handed Harry
the coat that
had faded and
shrunk because it had
been worn by Marcus
AND Johnny AND George.

They'd only got to the top of the hill when
the bike chain broke.
"Oh no!" cried Harry's mum.
"Oh no!" cried Marcus and Johnny and George.
"Oh no!" cried Harry.

"That bike's too old," said Harry's mum. "It's had it!
You'll have to walk, Harry. Never mind, you'll soon be
walking to big school every day with your brothers!"
"It's not fair!" Harry said.

Just before school started, it was Harry's fifth birthday.
The very best day of the year. After all, it was the
only time anyone gave Harry anything NEW!

The only trouble was, Marcus AND Johnny AND
George all wanted to play with Harry's new
things. But Harry didn't want them to.

Everything looked new,
and that was the way Harry
wanted it to stay.

But Harry did let Marcus and
Johnny and George play with
the hand-me-down toys.

"It's not fair. I had this bike for my fifth birthday and
Harry's got it for free!" said Marcus.

"It's not fair. I had
this skateboard for my fifth birthday and
Harry's got it for free!" said Johnny.

"It's not fair. I had this train set for my fifth birthday and Harry's got it for free!" said George.

"At least they were shiny and unscratched
when YOU had them!" cried Harry.

And then Harry's mum called,
"Stop it, you lot! Come on, Harry,
time to try on your school uniform!"
Harry knew exactly what was coming . . .

. . . worn-out grey trousers, holey school sweaters and knotted stringy ties!

The worst hand-me-downs of the lot!
They had been worn by Marcus AND Johnny
AND George for the last six years!

"Come on, Harry!" they all cried.
"Let's see what you look like!"

Harry sighed.
And then the miracle happened . . .

There, right in front of
Harry's eyes was . . .

a
brand-
new
shirt,

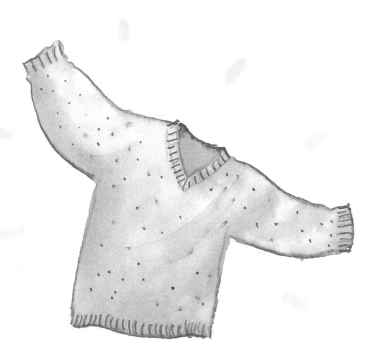

a
brand-
new
jumper,

and a
brand-new
skirt!

"Well, we couldn't have you going to
school looking like a **boy**,
could we, Harriet?" said her mum.

Harry couldn't believe it!
Her shirt was crisp and new-smelling,
her jumper didn't have a single hole,
her skirt was neatly pleated.

"Yippee!"

Harry cried.

She was so pleased,
   she didn't even mind that
      she had to wear the hand-me-down coat on top.

Harry looked **really smart** when she went off to school. All her brothers said so.

She even looked smart when she came back. She brought some new friends home to play.

They were amazed by her bedroom.
"You've got cars!" cried Julia.
"And a **garage!**" cried Anna.
"And a **train set!**" said Sarah.
"And **footballs!**" said Kate.
"I know, all boys' things, all tatty
and scratched," said Harry.

"I've never seen
so many toys!"
said Sarah.

"Do they
really all
belong to you?"
asked Kate.

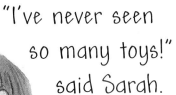

"I've always
wanted
a garage!"
said Anna.

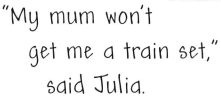

"My mum won't
get me a train set,"
said Julia.

"Aren't you lucky!"
cried everyone.
"It's not fair!"

Harry stared at them. Lucky? Her?
She looked around her. She did
have a lot of toys. She supposed
she was lucky. And if none of her
friends cared that they weren't
brand-new, why should she?

After all, they all worked . . .

. . . most of the time!

And even when they didn't,
she had plenty of help in
mending them!

And now, instead of saying,
"It's not fair!" Harry said,
"I'm Hand-me-down Harry!"
very proudly.